In the Sky

The Moon

by Carol Ryback
Reading consultant: Susan Nations, M.Ed., author/literacy coach/
consultant in literacy development

Please visit our web site at: www.earlyliteracy.cc
For a free color catalog describing Weekly Reader® Early Learning Library's
list of high-quality books, call 1-877-445-5824 (USA) or 1-800-387-3178 (Canada).
Weekly Reader® Early Learning Library's fax: (414) 336-0164.

Library of Congress Cataloging-in-Publication Data

Ryback, Carol.
    The moon / by Carol Ryback.
      p. cm. — (In the sky)
    Includes bibliographical references and index.
    ISBN 0-8368-6343-7 (lib. bdg.)
    ISBN 0-8368-6348-8 (softcover)
    1. Moon—Juvenile literature. I. Title.
    QB582.R93   2006
    523.3—dc22   2005026534

This edition first published in 2006 by
Weekly Reader® Early Learning Library
A Member of the WRC Media Family of Companies
330 West Olive Street, Suite 100
Milwaukee, WI 53212 USA

Copyright © 2006 by Weekly Reader® Early Learning Library

Series editor: Dorothy L. Gibbs
Editor: Barbara Kiely Miller
Art direction, cover and layout design: Tammy West
Photo research: Diane Laska-Swanke

Photo credits: Cover, title, NASA/JPL-Caltech; pp. 5, 6, 7, 11, 14 NASA; p. 9 Lick Observatory;
pp. 10, 19, 21 NASA Goddard Space Flight Center; p. 13 NASA Kennedy Space Center; pp. 16, 20
NASA Johnson Space Center; p. 17 © Ken Lucas/Visuals Unlimited

Printed in the United States of America

1 2 3 4 5 6 7 8 9 10 09 08 07 06

Table of Contents

On the cover and title page: Earth's dry, dusty Moon is covered with craters.

CHAPTER

A Light in the Night Sky

The Moon is easy to see in the night sky. It looks like a bright light that is much bigger than a star. The Moon travels across the sky from east to west. It follows a path in space called an **orbit**. The Moon's orbit makes a big circle around Earth.

The Moon does not make its own light. The Sun lights the Moon. From Earth, we see the part of the Moon that is lit up by the Sun. If the Sun's light did not fall on the Moon, we would not see the Moon in the night sky.

The Moon orbits Earth in twenty-nine and one-half days.

ORBIT

MOON

EARTH

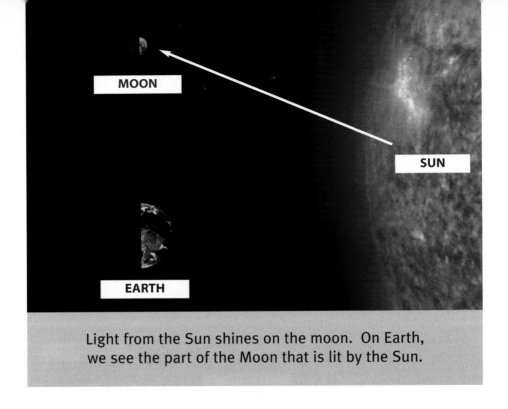

MOON

SUN

EARTH

Light from the Sun shines on the moon. On Earth,
we see the part of the Moon that is lit by the Sun.

The Moon is round, but it does not always look
round. It seems to slowly change shape from
week to week. The Moon's shape does not really
change. As the Sun lights up different parts of
the Moon, we see different shapes.

The many shapes of the Moon are called **phases**. The Moon has four phases. Each phase has a name. The names are the new Moon, the crescent Moon, the quarter Moon, and the full Moon.

The Moon's phases change slowly as the Moon orbits Earth.

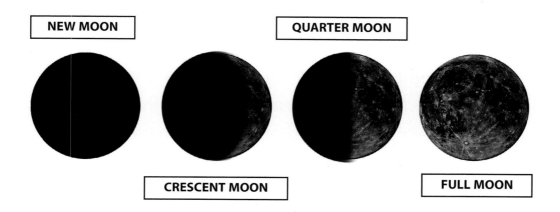

NEW MOON

QUARTER MOON

CRESCENT MOON

FULL MOON

CHAPTER

The Man in the Moon

Some people think they see a face when they look at the Moon. They call it the Man in the Moon. Of course, the Moon does not have a face. It is covered with rocks and dust that make different areas look dark or light.

The dark parts of the Moon are mostly flat rocks. Long ago, people thought the flat, dark areas of the Moon were oceans, or seas. They gave these places names such as the "Sea of Peace" and the "Sea of Clouds." We now know that there are no oceans on the Moon, but we still call the Moon's dark areas "seas."

Long ago, people thought the dark areas of the Moon were oceans.

An astronaut leaves a footprint in the
Moon's powdery soil.

The light parts of the Moon are mostly soil.
A layer of powdery, gray soil covers most of the
Moon. It covers the Moon's hills, mountains,
and craters.

Craters on the Moon look like big, round holes with high sides. They were made by huge space boulders that hit the Moon and bounced off. Most of the craters on the Moon are billions of years old.

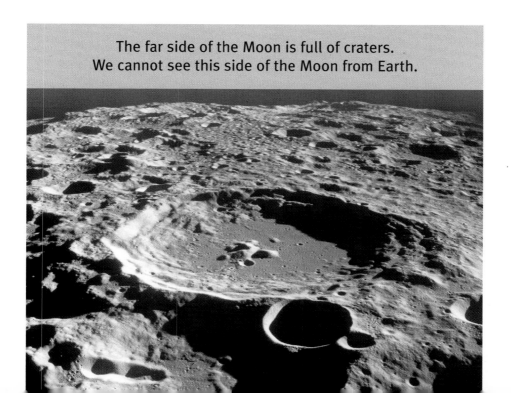

The far side of the Moon is full of craters.
We cannot see this side of the Moon from Earth.

CHAPTER 3

Light and Shadow

Sometimes, the Moon passes between Earth and the Sun. In this position, the Moon blocks the Sun's light so it does not reach Earth. Instead, the Moon's shadow falls on Earth. The Moon blocking the light of the Sun is called a **solar eclipse**.

Sometimes, Earth passes between the Sun and the Moon. Earth blocks the Sun's light so it does not reach the Moon. Instead, the shadow of Earth darkens the Moon. Earth's shadow covering all or part of the Moon is called a **lunar eclipse**.

Earth's shadow falls on the full Moon during a lunar eclipse.

We see only one side of the Moon from Earth. The side we cannot see is called the far side of the Moon. Spacecraft have taken pictures of the Moon's far side. The pictures show almost no flat areas. The far side of the Moon is covered with many craters.

Craters formed when large space boulders hit the far side of the Moon.

CHAPTER 4

A Strong Downward Pull

Earth is about four times bigger than the Moon. It also weighs a lot more than the Moon. Earth's size and weight cause a pull called **gravity**. Earth's gravity pulls on the Moon, which keeps the Moon in its orbit around Earth.

The Moon's weak gravity lets an astronaut jump
high — even in a heavy space suit.

The Moon has gravity, too. The Moon's gravity,
however, is much weaker than Earth's gravity.
If you weigh 100 pounds (45 kilograms) on Earth,
you would weigh only about 17 pounds (8 kg) on
the Moon. Just think how high you could jump!

The Moon's gravity is weak, but it still pulls on Earth. The Moon's gravity pulls on the water in Earth's oceans. This pull causes tides in the oceans. Tides are the changing water levels in the oceans. Water is deeper at high tide than at low tide.

The Moon's gravity pulls on Earth to cause tides in the oceans. At high tide, the water reaches the rocks. At low tide, the beach gets wider and you see more sand.

CHAPTER 5

A Trip to the Moon

The distance between Earth and the Moon is about 240,000 miles (385,000 kilometers). This distance is about the same as traveling from New York City to Los Angeles, California, one hundred times. If you could take a highway to the Moon, you would be driving for almost 143 days—without stopping! Spaceships travel much faster. Some spaceships can reach the Moon in only three days!

People who travel in space are called **astronauts**. Astronauts first landed on the Moon on July 20, 1969. While they were on the Moon, the astronauts took pictures and set up scientific tests. They also collected Moon rocks to carry back to Earth.

Astronaut Ed "Buzz" Aldrin was the second person to ever walk on the Moon. Astronaut Neil Armstrong was the first.

An astronaut explores the Moon on a lunar rover.

Six teams of astronauts visited the Moon at different times. Some of the teams brought along special cars, called **lunar rovers,** to drive on the Moon. The astronauts used the lunar rovers to help them explore the Moon. When the astronauts came back to Earth, they left the lunar rovers on the Moon.

One astronaut hit a golf ball on the Moon. The ball landed in a crater. The astronaut made the first hole in one on the Moon! The last time anyone walked on the Moon was in 1972. Someday, astronauts may visit the Moon again. Will you be one of them?

Who will be the next person to walk on the Moon?

Glossary

boulders — very large rocks

craters — round, bowl-shaped holes

crescent — a curved shape, like the letter C, with pointed tips

eclipse — a temporary shadow in space that blocks sunlight from reaching the Moon or a planet

lunar — having to do with the Moon

phases — a set of changes, such as changes in shape

solar — having to do with the Sun

tides — the rising and falling of ocean water levels that happen at certain times each day

For More Information

Books

The Moon. Seymour Simon (Simon & Schuster Children's Books)

Moon. Jump into Science (series). Steve Tomecek (National Geographic Children's Books)

Reaching for the Moon. Buzz Aldrin (HarperCollins)

So That's How the Moon Changes Shape! Rookie Read-About Science (series). Allan Fowler (Scholastic)

Web Sites

Earth's Moon — Our Favorite Satellite
solarsystem.nasa.gov/planets/profile.cfm?Object=Moon&Display=Kids
Explore NASA's Moon page for kids.

The Moon: Tides
www.enchantedlearning.com/subjects/astronomy/moon/Tides.shtml
Learn how the Moon's gravity causes Earth's tides.

Index

About the Author

Carol Ryback remembers saving her allowance to buy a school binder that featured the planets. She still finds outer space and other "scientific stuff" fascinating. A lifelong Wisconsin resident, Carol's favorite dog stars are golden retrievers Bailey, Merlin, and Harley Taylorson. When not stargazing, Carol likes to scuba dive.